JEN 9.95

W9-AUS-869

EAST NORTHPORT PUBLIC LIBR.
EAST NORTHPORT, NEW YOR

The
Mermaid's
Cape

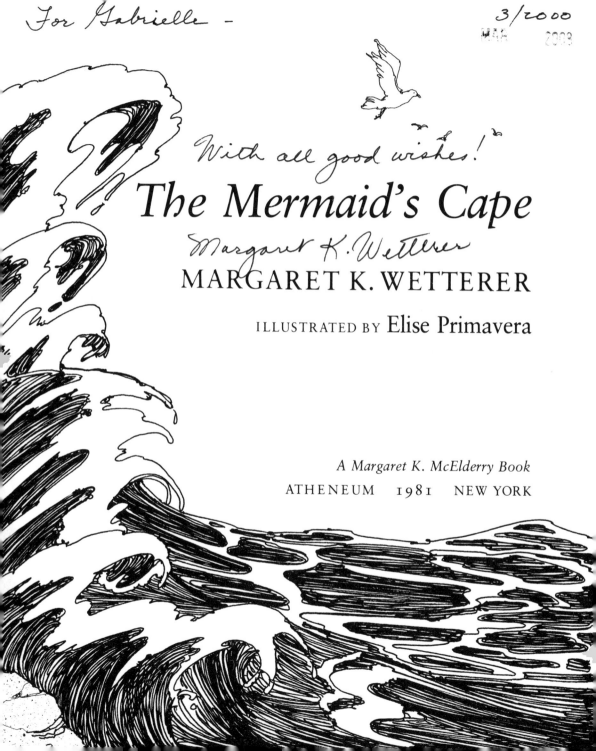

For Gabrielle — 3/2000

With all good wishes!

Margaret K. Wetterer

The Mermaid's Cape

MARGARET K. WETTERER

ILLUSTRATED BY Elise Primavera

A Margaret K. McElderry Book

ATHENEUM   1981   NEW YORK

LIBRARY OF CONGRESS CATALOGING IN PUBLICATION DATA

Wetterer, Margaret K
The mermaid's cape.

"A Margaret K. McElderry book."
SUMMARY: When he falls in love with a beautiful
mermaid who drifts in too close to shore, a young
Irish fisherman snatches up her shimmering cape
knowing that as long as he has it the mermaid can
never leave.
[1. Fairy tales.   2. Mermaids—Fiction]
I. Primavera, Elise.   II. Title.
PZ8.W54Me   [E]   80–20338
ISBN 0–689–50197–8

Text copyright © 1981 by Margaret K. Wetterer
Illustrations copyright © 1981 by Elise Primavera
All rights reserved
Published simultaneously in Canada by McClelland & Stewart, Ltd.
Composition by Connecticut Printers, Incorporated
Bloomfield, Connecticut
Printed by Halliday Lithograph Corporation
West Hanover, Massachusetts
Bound by A. Horowitz & Sons/Bookbinders
Fairfield, New Jersey
First Edition

For Kitty, Jim & Jack & their father
M.K.W.

For my parents
E.P.

ONCE UPON A TIME in a lonely cottage on an island off the west coast of Ireland, there lived a handsome young fisherman. Every day the young fisherman and two men from the nearby village set out in a curragh to fish. They rowed the boat out beyond the foaming breakers, out beyond the rocks where sleek seals played, out to where silver fish swam in the green-black sea. There the fishermen put down their nets. Sometimes they were lucky and caught more fish then they could carry home in the curragh. Sometimes they caught nothing.

In the spring of the year, when the night sea churned with the rush of spawning fish, the young fisherman and his companions often went to fish in the evening just as the sun was setting. They would fish all night under the cold white moon.

Early one spring morning, after they had fished the long night through, the fishermen rowed into a sheltered cove and carried their curragh high onto the pebbly beach. There they stowed their nets in a shack on the beach. The other fishermen hurried home with their night's catch. But the young fisherman, who had no wife or child awaiting him in his lonely cottage, lingered behind to mend one of his nets.

No sooner had the other fishermen left the cove than a beautiful green-eyed mermaid came drifting in toward the beach. She came with the waves, floating upon them, tossed about by them, leaning back against them with her arms outstretched. The waves pushed her landward as they swirled and broke around her. She waved to the barking seals as she floated past their rocks. She laughed merrily and called to the sea birds that gathered to welcome her.

The young fisherman, hidden in the shadow of the shack, gazed entranced as the mermaid rose from the surf and stepped lightly out upon the beach. It was true, he saw, that mermaids in that part of the world had legs. She wore a long blue gown, tied at the waist with a golden rope, and around her shoulders, flowing down to her heels, hung a shimmering sea-green cape, the magic cape of a mermaid.

The young fisherman watched the mermaid climb nimbly upon a great rock at the water's edge. She dropped the cape from her shoulders and sat upon it and began to comb her tangled dark brown hair. As she combed her hair, she sang a song in a voice so sweet that the birds stopped their calling to listen.

The young fisherman watched and listened too. He had never seen anyone as beautiful or heard a song as lovely. He felt his heart would burst with love and longing if he could not marry the mermaid. But he knew that a mermaid would never leave the sea willingly. She would never give up the carefree life of eternal youth in the sea for the hard life of a mortal wife full of care and toil.

"I will steal her away from the sea," said the fisherman to himself. "I will make her my wife and love her, and surely she will grow to love me."

Silently, stealthily, swiftly he crept up behind the mermaid. He was almost upon her when the gulls saw him and shrieked in warning. The mermaid leaped up in fright, sprang from the rock, and rushed down into the sea. The gulls swooped and gathered up the cape, which in her haste the mermaid had left behind her, but the fisherman snatched it from them.

The mermaid called to him from the sea, "Please, give me back my cape. Please, give me back my cape. It is nothing at all to you, but it is all in all to me." And she cried and pleaded in a piteous manner. The birds and the seals took up the sad note and seemed to be begging with her.

Though his heart was moved with pity, for he was a kindly man, still the young fisherman would not give her the cape. He knew that while he had the cape he had power over the mermaid, who could not live and breathe in the sea without it.

After a time the mermaid saw that her tears and her pleadings were in vain. Sadly and slowly she rose from the surf and stepped wearily out upon the beach.

"Come with me," said the young fisherman. "I will make you my wife, and I will love you always," and he gently took the mermaid by her small white hand.

Sadly and slowly the mermaid followed the young fisherman home.

That night, while the mermaid slept, the fisherman rolled up the cape. It seemed almost alive and moving in his hands as if it, too, wanted to be free from his grasp. With great difficulty he squeezed it tightly into a small ball and hid it behind a loose stone in the kitchen fireplace.

Now friends and neighbors warned the fisherman not to marry the mermaid. "This creature from the sea is not of human kind," they said. "There are many fine girls in the village who would gladly be your wife. Marry one of them."

The young fisherman wanted no one but the mermaid.

The parish priest warned the fisherman not to marry the mermaid. "Sorrow will come of it," he predicted. "It is wrong to take a wild creature of nature and burden her with the cares of a mortal. Look for someone like yourself to marry."

The young fisherman wanted no one but her.

The parish priest then asked the mermaid, "Do you wish to marry this man?"

"I must do as he wishes," she answered sadly; and that was so. As long as the fisherman had the cape, he had power over her. She could not go back to the sea without it, and she would not leave the place where it was.

So they were married the following Sunday, and all in the village were invited to the wedding. There was good food and drink and music, but the mermaid would not eat or drink or sing at her wedding.

As time passed the mermaid proved to be a careful, skillful wife. She cooked and cleaned and tended the garden; but she never smiled, she never laughed, she never sang a note as she went about her chores. Often in the morning, just as the dawn was breaking, she would wander down to the sheltered cove and stare wistfully out at the sea. Sometimes when the wind was high, she would listen, listen as if voices from the sea were calling her.

The fisherman loved the mermaid, and it grieved him to see her so unhappy. He tried in every way to please her. He searched for pretty shells and fragrant flowers to delight her. He brought her satin ribbons for her hair. But the one thing that he knew would truly make her happy, he would not give her. He would not give her back her cape, and with it, her freedom.

Seven years passed, and at last a child was born to the mermaid and the fisherman. For the first time since she left the sea, the mermaid smiled. She smiled at her newborn son.

Never since time began was there a handsomer child. He had red hair like his father and green eyes like his mother. He was lively and merry, quick to learn and quick to laugh.

They called their son Brendan after the great sailor-saint. Often in the evening, when Brendan was restless and could not sleep, his mother would sit by his bed in the corner of the kitchen and sing to him. The mermaid sang a song in a voice so sweet that peace flowed into the hearts of all who heard her. And Brendan slept. The fisherman smiled and said to himself, "At last the mermaid is happy."

The mermaid taught Brendan many things. By the time he could walk and talk, Brendan knew the name and call of every sea bird. When he was five years old he could swim to the rocks and play with the seals. His mother taught him to read the stars and the tides and the winds. He could predict changes of weather, the migration of birds, and the movement of fish. She told him about all the creatures of the sea. She spoke of the fair-skinned mermaids and of the merrows, the green-skinned men who live under the sea. "Mermaids have magic capes and merrows have magic caps that enable them to live and breathe beneath the water."

"How do you know such things, Mother?" Brendan asked.

"I just know," answered the mermaid.

The fisherman, too, taught Brendan many things. He taught him how to build a curragh and how to row it in calm seas or rough. He showed him how to make

a net and how to mend one. When Brendan was seven years old, he began to fish with his father. Whenever Brendan put down a net, it was never drawn up empty. Other fishermen might fish and catch nothing, but Brendan and his father always caught as many fish as they could carry home in the curragh. For three years this went on, and the fisherman and his family prospered. The people in the village saw this good luck and murmured among themselves, remembering that Brendan's mother was a mermaid.

One day the fisherman said to Brendan, "Your
mother is growing old too soon. Her hands are rough
and careworn. At the end of the day her steps are slow
and weary. Her hair is turning gray. She was never
meant for such a hard life. We are earning good
money fishing. I will hire a girl from the village to help
your mother with the work of the house and garden."

"And, Father, I will save the money you give me for helping you, and I will surprise Mother with a beautiful present. It will show her how much I love her. Perhaps I will buy tortoiseshell combs for her hair or a necklace of pink and white pearls," declared Brendan.

So the next day the fisherman went off to inquire of some women in the village about a girl to help his wife.

After he left, Brendan looked around the house for a good place to hide his money. "I must find a hiding place where no one would think of looking, a place where I can save enough money to buy Mother a wonderful surprise."

He thought he might keep his money under the bed in the corner of the kitchen, but no, his mother would find it when she swept under there.

He thought of the rafters under the thatched roof, but no, that was too hard for him to reach.

Then he thought of a place where no one would think of looking, a place that was easy to reach. Delighted with himself, he pulled out a loose stone in the kitchen fireplace. To his amazement, as he pulled out the stone, a wrinkled green cloth fell out. Brendan spread the cloth on the floor. It felt damp and warm and it smelled of the sea; and it sparkled and glistened as he touched it.

"What can this be?" he wondered.

"Father!" Brendan started to call, but then he remembered his father was out. Perhaps his mother would know.

Brendan found his mother on her knees in the garden, planting new cabbage. "Mother, what is this?" he asked.

The mermaid stopped her work and looked at her son and smiled. Then she looked at what he was holding.

With a cry of joy the mermaid sprang to her feet; she seized the cape and flung it round her shoulders.

Brendan stared for a moment in wonder and fear as his mother ran out the garden gate and off down the road through the village. "Mother!" he cried and ran after her.

The fisherman walking home heard a ringing, merry laugh. He stared for a moment in wonder and fear as his wife ran past him on the road, and Brendan after her, down toward her home in the sea. "Wife!" he cried, and he, too, ran after her.

Half the village joined in the chase, but the mermaid outran them all. As she ran, the cape billowed out behind her, floating, flapping, dancing in the sunlight like something alive and free. As she ran, the years dropped from her; her green eyes glistened; and her dark hair tumbled down her shoulders. She was beautiful. She was joyful. She was young again.

Laughing all the while, the mermaid plunged head-
long into the sea.

"Come back, woman," called the priest. "You belong now with your husband and child."

But the mermaid swam on.

"Come back, dear wife," called the fisherman. "Your son and I need you."

But the mermaid swam on.

"Come back, Mother," called Brendan. "We love you. We love you." And he ran into the surf after his mother.

The mermaid turned. "Stop!" she commanded. "You cannot go where I go." She gazed for a moment at Brendan and then at the fisherman before sinking down into the green-black sea.

Brendan and his father waited and watched for a long while, but they saw no more of the mermaid. Sadly and slowly they left the cove. Sadly and slowly they walked back to their lonely cottage.

The priest sighed. "I warned him not to marry the mermaid."

"We knew no good would come of it," said the friends and neighbors.

That night Brendan lay on his bed in the corner of the kitchen. He could not sleep. Through stinging tears he watched his father slumped in a chair before the dying fire.

Just when Brendan felt his heart would burst with sorrow and longing, he heard a song on the wind. At first it was faint and far away, but then it grew clearer and closer. Brendan and his father scarcely breathed as they listened. The mermaid was nearby and singing. She sang them a song, a song of love, a song of their life together and of the happiness the mermaid had brought them. She sang them a song in a voice so sweet that their cares dissolved like sea foam.

The fisherman knelt beside Brendan's bed. He was smiling. "Your mother is happy now, and she still loves us, son," he whispered.

"Yes, Father." Brendan nodded. "We will always love one another."

And Brendan closed his eyes, and as the mermaid's song filled the cottage, he went peacefully to sleep.

MAR 2008

Northport-East Northport Public Library

To view your patron record from a computer, click on
the Library's homepage: **www.nenpl.org**

You may:
- request an item be placed on hold
- renew an item that is overdue
- view titles and due dates checked out on your card
- view your own outstanding fines

**185 Larkfield Road
East Northport, NY 11731
631-261-2313**